Here Comes
SANTA
CAT

Here Comes
SANTA

CAT

by
DEBORAH UNDERWOOD

pictures by
CLAUDIA RUEDA

PUFFIN BOOKS

Hey, Santa!

Have you seen Cat?

Cat! I didn't even
recognize you.

Why are you dressed
like Santa?

So you can give yourself
a present?

Oh, Cat. Santa will bring
you a present, won't he?

No? Why not?

Ah. I see your problem.

But are you *sure* you want to be Santa? Santa has to climb down chimneys.

Can you do that?

Well, maybe you'll get
the hang of it.

But Cat, Santa has magic reindeer.
How will *you* fly?

A jet pack?

Do you even know how to use a—

Ouch.

Cat, this is silly. Besides, Santa doesn't give gifts to himself.

He gives them to other people.

Well, I'm sorry, but
that's just the way it is.

Instead of being Santa,
why don't you just try
to be nice?

You're worried it's too late?

It's never too late!

What's a nice thing you could do?

Go Christmas caroling?
Great!

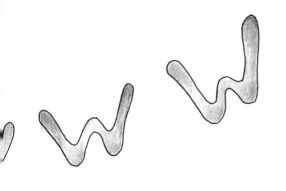

Uh, Cat?

Maybe something else.

You're going to give presents
to children?

That's wonderful!

What happened?

The children didn't *want*
the presents?

What were you giving them?

Ah.

Any other ideas?

Maybe ones that don't
involve fish?

Yes! It would be very nice if you helped decorate the tree in the town square.

Good going, Cat!

Have fun!

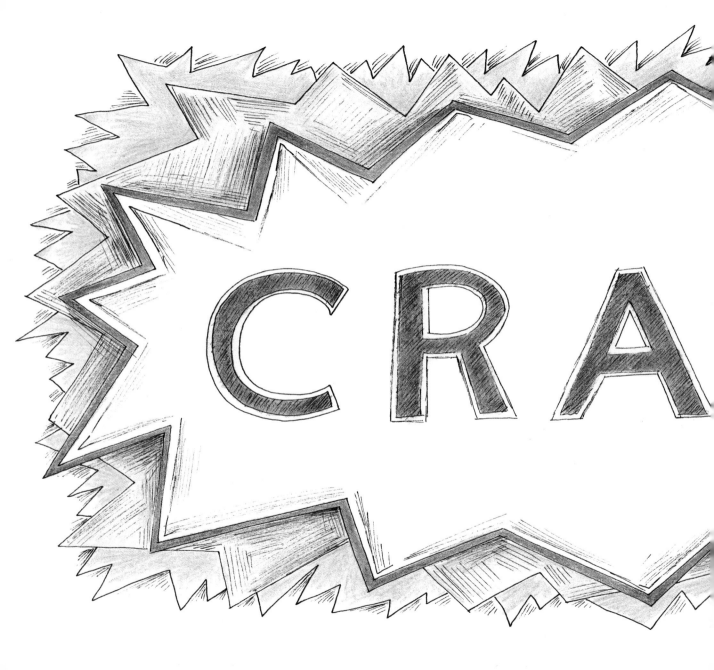

Wow.

Oh, Cat.

I'm sure Santa is glad you tried.

I am too.

In fact, I have a present for
you myself...

Two cans of your favorite
fancy cat food!

Well, my goodness! Who's this?

I wonder what that poor kitten wants, Cat.

Any ideas?

Cat, do you realize what
just happened?

You did something nice!

Hey, do you hear that?

JiNGLE
JiNGLE
JiNGLE

Look! It's Santa!

And he *does* have a present
for you!

Wow! An official
Santa's Helper suit!

Cat!

Where are you going?

You have a present
for Santa?

Nice, Cat. Very nice.

For Lissa, Lynn, and Elizabeth —D.U.
For Sophie, the cat —C.R.

PUFFIN BOOKS
An imprint of Penguin Random House LLC
375 Hudson Street
New York, New York 10014

First published in the United States of America by Dial Books for Young Readers,
an imprint of Penguin Group (USA) LLC, 2014
Published by Puffin Books, an imprint of Penguin Random House LLC, 2016

Text copyright © 2014 by Deborah Underwood
Pictures copyright © 2014 by Claudia Rueda

THE LIBRARY OF CONGRESS HAS CATALOGED THE DIAL BOOKS FOR YOUNG READERS EDITION AS FOLLOWS:
Underwood, Deborah.
Here comes Santa Cat / by Deborah Underwood ; pictures by Claudia Rueda.
pages cm
Summary: "Cat wants off Santa's naughty list and makes several valiant attempts, but this 'being nice' business is trickier than he thought"—Provided by publisher.
ISBN 978-0-8037-4100-3 (hardcover)
[1. Cats—Fiction. 2. Santa Claus—Fiction. 3. Gifts—Fiction.
4. Conduct of life—Fiction. 5. Humorous stories.]
I. Rueda, Claudia, illustrator. II. Title.
PZ7.U4193Hd 2014   [E]—dc23   2013035538

Puffin Books ISBN 978-0-425-28795-8

Printed in the USA

10 9 8 7 6 5 4 3 2

THE ART WAS MADE WITH INK AND COLOR
PENCILS ON WHITE PAPER, SURROUNDED
BY HUNDREDS OF CATS (INK CATS!).